School Is Not For Me,
Jeremy James Conor McGee

*A Young Boy's Journey with
Learning Disabilities*

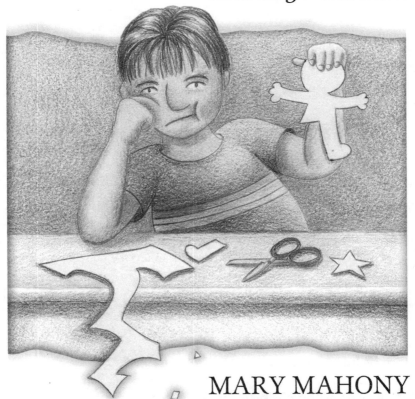

MARY MAHONY

Illustrations by Sarah Frederick

REDDING PRESS • BELMONT

D1227587

Printed in the United States of America. No part of the contents of this book may be reproduced without written permission of the publisher.

Susan A. Pasternack, Editor
Illustrations by Sarah Frederick
Cover and interior design © TLC Graphics, *www.TLCGraphics.com*
Portrait on page 51 Joe Demb Photography,
59 Louise Rd., Belmont, MA 02478

Printed by Bang Printing, Brainerd, MN
10 9 8 7 6 5 4 3 2 1
Fiction
RL: 3-5
Library of Congress Control Number: 2009921678
ISBN: 978-0-9658879-4-6

Dedication

*To all students, especially those whom I have taught,
who deal with the daily challenges of learning difficulties
and have the courage to persevere*

School Is Not For Me, Jeremy James Connor McGee is an entertaining and meaningful read for students, teachers, and parents. Through the eyes of a student (Jeremy) with learning challenges, the reader is sensitized to his feelings, worries, and needs. Jeremy provides instruction for adults who learn to "tune in" to children, inculcate them with hope and positive beliefs, and adapt approaches while always persevering with passion. All of this with good humor, too! Apparently, the Jeremys in schools have taught the Marys what works and what doesn't. Not all Jeremys fare as well in real life. But as more adults (particularly teachers) read and embrace the book's messages, we'll witness a greater number of successful and happy Jeremys. Jeremy's plight hits a nerve with me, as I struggled as a third grader in the most stressful time of my childhood. I was Mary's colleague and supervisor for nearly twenty years. This book reflects her insight, unwavering commitment, and joy of the teaching profession. Bravo!

EDWARD ORENSTEIN
Retired Collaborative Executive Director
and Special Education Administrator

For the Student Reader

If you could choose one place that you would really love to be, it might or might not be school. Like you, Jeremy James Conor McGee is not sure that school will ever be a place that he likes to be. His story may remind you of some of your own experiences in school or of those of one of your siblings or friends. Maybe you are Jeremy, and if so, now you are famous because someone has written a book about you. There is a little bit of Jeremy in all of us. Sometimes it is hard to remember that school is the key that opens many doors and ultimately gives us the toolbox we may need to follow our dreams. For Jeremy, his dream is to go to the moon, and I believe that someday he will get there. We all need to have a dream. No dream is too silly or too far-reaching. Whatever your dream is, don't ever let it go. Just keep thinking, "I can do it, I can do it, I can do it," and, hopefully, someday you will.

For the Adult Reader

This is a story that is equally meaningful to children and adults, since Jeremy's feelings and insights into learning disabilities are not unlike those of many students who struggle for both acceptance and success in school. The ability and desire to read and to perform other academic tasks are important keys that open many doors. It is essential that we, as parents and educators, remember to give our children the best toolbox we can to prepare them for the future with the hope that, like Jeremy, they will dare to dream and become passionate about something. Today, the world is full of "passionless" students and adults who have no dreams or lack the tools to develop and pursue their dreams. Be there for them in any way you can so that just maybe their dreams will come true.

A special thanks to my mother,
Patricia MacGuire Sunderland,
for encouraging me to pursue my passion for writing

Chapter One

I LIVE IN A HOUSE THAT IS PRETTY MUCH LIKE LOTS OF OTHER HOUSES: kitchen, bedrooms, family room, porch, driveway with basketball net, and a small yard. I have two goldfish, John and Joseph, a brother named Jacob who is four years older than me, and a dog named Foolish, whom I consider to be my other brother. Foolish is older than Jacob but not quite as old as my parents.

My brother, Jacob, is really smart and does everything perfectly. He's nice to me most of the time, but I always feel that I can never do anything as good as he does. Mom and Dad are always asking him to help me with stuff. My dad is a scientist. My mom used to work in a lab near my dad but stayed home after I was born. They like to talk about science and experiments at home, especially with Jacob. If you want to know a big secret, I am very tired of that. Jacob has tons of friends and he always gets phone calls and play dates. I have one very special friend named Joey and that's all.

Joey lives about five minutes from me and we have been friends since we were babies. Our moms met at the park and ever since then Joey and I have played together all the time. If I'm not playing with Joey, I'm goofing around with Foolish. I tell Foolish everything because I know he will never repeat what I say.

When we're not home, Foolish has to go into a crate to keep him out of trouble. It looks more like "dog jail" to me. Mom used to take Foolish to dog training school but instead of Foolish jumping over the barrier, Mom did, because Foolish was running around getting the other dogs excited. Mom really *did* think

Foolish was jumping with her. Finally they told her that Foolish couldn't go back to dog training school anymore. They even gave Mom this fancy paper saying that Foolish finished his training, but he really didn't. Dad says that in regular schools that would never, ever be allowed to happen. It was a very dishonest thing to do to poor Foolish.

Let me tell you about my life beginning when I was almost four years old and just starting preschool. My mom went back to work and so there were big changes at home. My whole family was always rushing around and complaining about being late. "Hurry up" and "late" were the big words in our house. It was pretty wild. Poor Foolish was the saddest about Mom going back to work. He had to live in that big crate all day long. Each morning, when we said goodbye, he had very sad eyes.

Joey and I went to the same preschool so we were both Green Frogs. Our room had green frogs everywhere, but they weren't real. Our room also had a big fish tank, a case with gerbils in it, and a huge wooden fort that everyone got to climb. When we went out in the hallway, we had to line up on green frogs that were pasted all over the floor. Joey said that our teacher, Mrs. King, should have been called Mrs. Green Frog, but I guess she liked her real name better.

Every day Joey went home at lunchtime, but I had to go to Kiddie Care because my parents were at work. Joey's mom promised me that sometimes I could go home and play with Joey after school. Joey had no sisters or brothers, but he did have a big brown bunny rabbit with long floppy ears and a parrot that said silly things. The first time I ever met his parrot, the bird yelled out "You stink!" Joey and I laughed really hard.

Chapter Two

THE PRESCHOOL WHERE JOEY AND I WERE GREEN FROGS WAS THE same one that my brother Jacob went to before me.

"Wait till they find out I am not at all like Jacob," I thought to myself before I started. "It sure is going to be a lot different with me."

It didn't take the teachers very long to figure that out. It was hard for me to get all my stuff in my cubby and sit down on the rug on time. At first Joey waited for me, but Mrs. King told him that he had to go in and sit down. I was always the last one on the rug, so I almost never got to sit next to Joey. That really made me sad. Mrs. King kept coming over to me or asking one of her helpers to. Every morning when I got there I heard Mrs. King say, "Looks like Jeremy may need help again." I wanted to tell her that I didn't need help. I just needed more time.

I talked only to Joey in school. Other kids might not have understood what I was saying because the words didn't always come out of my mouth the right way. Joey always knew what I meant, though. Even if I didn't say anything, he knew what I was thinking.

Joey wasn't like the other kids in school. He never bothered me with silly questions; he just liked to play. We would make up moon games at free play and Joey always thought up funny things that could happen up there on the moon. My dream then and now is to visit the moon and Joey says that he would like to go with me. He was the very first person I knew who really thought that someday we could go to the moon for a vacation.

If Joey hadn't been there, I wouldn't have liked preschool at all. Each morning when I woke up, I just lay in my bed thinking, "School is not for me!" I wasn't very good at anything and I could never do stuff like the other kids. Each time I had to cut something out, the other kids would tell me that I had just chopped off the head or the leg or arm. Mrs. King would help me and another kid in our class because that girl was a bad cutter-outer, too. I would have liked school better if I could have played with Joey all the time and made up games, like pretending that I was doing pushups on the moon or directing all the moon creatures to find a special star to live on. I would rather have gone to the moon than to school.

At dinner my dad always wanted to know what we did in school and I never had much to tell. One night I decided to talk about the moon game that Joey and I played. Before I even finished, Jacob started telling me all this stuff about the moon and ended by saying that people couldn't *do* pushups there. My dad looked at Jacob with this big smile on his face and then he looked over at me with sad eyes. Jacob knew everything. "Maybe I'm just not as smart as Jacob," I thought.

Lots of nights I could hear my parents talking in their bedroom about how hard school was for me. I never told them that I could hear what they were saying. I just lay there in my bed and listened. I really wanted to tell them to stop talking about me and talk about somebody else, but then I wouldn't have known what they were thinking.

As long as I had Joey, I was happy. I kept telling my parents that I was having fun in school because I knew that's what they wanted to hear.

But after a while I started to like some of the things we did in preschool. At Thanksgiving we made turkey soup and had our own Thanksgiving dinner. We all had special hats and pretended that we had just landed at this special place called Plymouth Rock. The teacher called us Pilgrims and told us a story about why all these people called Pilgrims went on a big boat across a very big ocean to get here. I liked dressing up and pretending that I was someone else because it made me feel really important. I also knew what it was like to want to be somewhere else where they could do better. I sometimes wished that I could go somewhere else and do better.

I also liked the holiday cooking part at preschool, but I didn't like all the cutting and drawing we did for all the other holidays that come during the year. We even had to do a special party for this animal called a "groundhog," and everyone had to make a picture of him coming out of a hole in the ground. Joey made groundhog noises the whole morning until Mrs. King said he had to stop. I thought Joey made a good groundhog!

During the winter we had this big, big snowstorm and we didn't have to go to preschool for a few days. Joey's mom invited me over to play with him because my mom and dad had to work. We built all kinds of snow forts and pretended that they were made of moon flakes that had special powers and could get us to the moon. I made Joey promise that he would not tell Jacob or anyone else about our game because they would say that there was no such thing as a moon flake.

One really muddy day in the spring my whole class had to go outside to dig some dirt to put in a cup so we could plant a seed in it. Mrs. King told us that we would each have a bean growing from it to give to our mothers for Mother's Day. "What is my mother going to do with one bean?" I thought to myself. Joey said that if we gave them to just one of our mothers at least that mom would have two beans. Oh, beans, shmeans! I thought it was a silly gift!

Chapter Three

MY PRESCHOOL YEAR WAS ALMOST OVER AND ONE NIGHT AT DINNER, just before school ended, my mom and dad said that we were going to go visit kindergarten. Jacob got all excited and told me what a cool place it was. "Cool, shmool," I thought to myself.

Then it happened. Jacob yelled out, "Sure is going to be hard for you to go to a school without Joey." Mom and Dad gave Jacob bad looks, but my eyes had already gotten watery. I couldn't even talk.

Mom looked over at me and said, "Jeremy, all the kids that live on Joey's street go to another school in our town. I know that makes you feel really sad, but you will make lots of new friends in kindergarten and you can still play with Joey on the weekends."

"Weekends, shmeekends," I thought. "I don't want to go to school if Joey can't be there. He's the only thing I like about school." Then I quietly got up from the table and went over to Foolish. He was lying in his crate with the door open. I crawled into the crate with him and put my head on his back. I could feel his tail thumping against my leg. Foolish knew just how to make me feel better.

When I woke up the next morning, I couldn't remember how I had made it up to bed. I didn't feel much like getting up because I didn't want to visit kindergarten. "Maybe if I go to the same kindergarten as Jacob, it will make me smart," I thought. Then Mom came rushing into my bedroom and told me she was running late and that I had to get up and get dressed and hurry downstairs for breakfast. My dad couldn't help out because he had gone into work early so that he could leave his office early to join us for the kindergarten visit. Mom explained that Joey's mom was going to pick me up and drive me to preschool. She had taken me a few other times when my parents needed help.

Most of the time, I loved it when I could ride to preschool with Joey but today was different. I didn't even want to go to preschool, I just wanted to lie on the floor with Foolish and be sad. Why didn't anybody understand that?

When Joey's mom pulled up I didn't go running out the door. Mom tried to rush me along, but I took my time. As soon as I got into the car, I could tell that Joey's mom knew something was up because she kept trying to make me happy. Joey just looked at me and rolled his eyes up in back of his head each time she said something. It made me laugh and I kind of forgot about kindergarten.

When preschool ended that day, Mrs. King told me that my dad was going to pick me up at Kiddie Care. I lined up on the green frogs with the other Kiddie Care kids and went to lunch. When we sat down, I hardly ate anything. I kept thinking about Joey and going to the moon. "How can we plan our moon trip if we have to go to different schools?" I wondered. "This new school is going to be a big problem for me."

Dad picked me up later in the afternoon and told me that Mom would meet us at kindergarten. When we got to the school, Mom was waiting for us at the door so we could all go in together. We went into a big room full of moms and dads and kids my age. A tall lady spoke to us. She was the principal and her name was Mrs. Bunn. Jacob used to call her the "Big Whopper" like the big bun that comes with your hamburger at Burger King. Mom and Dad sent Jacob to his room that night.

Mrs. Bunn divided us up into groups and we each had a teacher in charge of our group who took us down to kindergarten. Our moms and dads had to wait in the big room with Mrs. Bunn.

A lot of the kids in my group looked much bigger than me and they talked and talked all the way down to the classroom. One of them, a girl, kept talking at me, but I just looked down at the floor and didn't answer. She was a big pain. Then the teacher said something to me and she was talking much too fast. I started to feel like *everybody* was talking at me. It put me in a bad mood.

When we got to the classroom, there were tables with things to do and more big people watching us. I heard the teacher who brought us say to the lady at my table "kind of quiet," and I thought she was talking about me. I didn't like that at all because she said it as if that was a problem. I ended up staying at the Play-Doh table the whole time. The teacher kept asking me if I wanted to go to the drawing table, but I sure wasn't going to draw for them. I was afraid they'd say, "can't draw good" and "kind of quiet."

I was really happy when I saw my mom and dad coming in to rescue me. The teacher came over and told Mom that I had had a wonderful time and made all sorts of things with my Play-Doh. Wrong! I made a flat-headed moon man who had short legs and no arms. No one even knew what he was. I didn't think it was so wonderful at all and I could not wait to leave. "What was that teacher thinking?" I asked myself.

When we got home that night, Jacob took off on kindergarten at the dinner table as if he wanted to go back there again himself. It seemed like everyone was excited about kindergarten except me. "Maybe they should all go back to kindergarten and I'll just stay home and play with Foolish," I kept thinking.

The next day I talked to Joey about my kindergarten visit. He said that he had to go see his kindergarten, too, but he didn't know when. I told him about how all the kids were talking at me and how much I hated that. Joey just looked at me for a minute and then he said, "Let's go to the moon, Jeremy."

Just before preschool ended some people from my new kindergarten came to meet me. They said they were just stopping by to visit my preschool, but I didn't believe them. They followed me around all morning, even though they wanted me to think they weren't. Even Joey asked me about them. I didn't like them being there at all.

At dinner that night I almost told Mom and Dad about them, but then I looked over at Jacob and decided it was not a very good idea.

Preschool ended with a fun ice-cream-cone party, except they put mine in a bowl upside down and I could hardly get to the ice cream because the cone was in the way. Even Joey asked me why they had put mine in a dish. When my ice cream started melting it began dripping on the floor because I was tilting the bowl to get the ice cream out from under the cone. One of the teacher-helpers kept telling me to hold the bowl straight. She kept saying that I better hurry up and finish it soon because ice cream melts. "Duh!" I thought to myself. "I know that!" If someone had not put the cone on top of my ice cream I might have been able to eat it faster! I felt like everyone was looking at me wondering why I had to eat mine out of a dish. That was my last memory of preschool. Not a good one at all.

Joey and I had a play date the day after school ended and his mom took us to the Discovery Park a few towns away. It was perfect. While Joey's mom sat on a bench and watched, Joey and I played with weights, made paint designs, and worked on a balance experiment. We climbed all over the dinosaur in the outside park and had lunch in the belly of a big plastic ape. It was a great day and I didn't want it ever to end. When it did, Joey's mom promised to call me for a play date with Joey over the summer. That made me really happy.

Chapter Four

THE SUMMER AFTER PRESCHOOL, FOR THE FIRST TIME EVER, MY PAR-
ents rented a house on Cape Cod for three weeks. They said that
they had a little extra money since Mom was working again.
The bad part was that after our Cape Cod vacation, Jacob and I
would be going to day camp while our parents were at work. I
loved the vacation part but I wasn't excited about going to camp
when my parents went back to work. "Work, shmirk!" I thought
to myself.

The first few days at the beach were awesome. Jacob and I
built sand castles while Mom sat in her chair reading and watching us. Then one day Jacob decided he wanted to swim rather
than build sand castles and Mom jumped up from her chair all
excited. Usually my mom is kind of calm and always really nice.

"Jeremy, let's teach you how to swim," she called out as she grabbed my hand and headed for the water. "Your dad can help out on the weekends, but I will get you started."

It turned out I made a better anchor than a float. No matter how hard I tried, I could not get myself to stay on top, and each time I sank I got a mouthful of this awful-tasting salt water. Then my mom got another very scary idea. "Jacob," she called. "Come help me teach Jeremy how to swim."

Jacob arrived in a flash, all set to make me this amazing swimmer. Remember, Jacob is good at *everything* he does, even swimming. Mom held onto my arms while Jacob went underwater and kept me afloat. When he ran out of air, he just let go, I would sink, and the show would begin all over again.

Pretty soon even the people swimming near me got into the act and I had my own cheering squad. Finally Jacob got tired and Mom decided that was enough for one day. I was so happy to sit on the beach again, but I was sure people would remember me as "the boy who didn't learn how to swim."

"Maybe tomorrow, Jeremy," people said as they left the beach, patting me on the back as they walked away.

"Oh no," I thought to myself, they *even* know my name!

The swimming lessons went on for days and days and finally our vacation ended and I still did not know how to swim. I could see the look of failure on my parents' faces and Jacob made a rap, which he thankfully left at the beach: "Be a float, not a moat. Come on Jeremy, float like a boat!"

When we got home, I was sad that I hadn't sent Joey a postcard from Cape Cod. I kept hoping that we would have a play date, but as soon as we got home day camp began. Camp was just okay and so was my counselor. If we didn't want to go into the pool on our own, we didn't have to and so I didn't, but I *did* have to take the swimming lessons. There were lots of games to play but I mostly did things by myself. I didn't meet anyone like Joey and so I just watched the other kids and sometimes joined a game with the help of my counselor. I was so tired by the end of the day that usually I fell asleep on the bus on the way home and Jacob had to wake me up. I really, really missed Joey.

Just before summer ended Joey came back from his vacation and called for a play date. I liked it better at Joey's house because it was just Joey and me and we could get our moon men ready to blast off. Jacob always called them "loony" moonie men!

When I got to Joey's that day, he was all excited because he had a little kiddie pool in his backyard that his mom had filled with water. I was glad that the water wasn't very deep. We splashed around and had cool water fights. Then Joey got a scary idea. Since his whole yard was fenced in, he said it would be okay to bring out Henry, his pet rabbit, and give him a swim. Joey's mom was busy cooking in the kitchen when Joey and I cornered Henry and took him outside. Joey could hardly keep Henry from jumping out of his arms, and when we got outside Joey lost his grip and Henry landed, head first, right in the kiddie pool. His big floppy ears went flat in the water. He kept trying and trying to get out, but it was too slippery. Henry was one very unhappy rabbit! Worse than that, Joey's mom heard the big splash and came out looking like a very unhappy mom. We were in big trouble!

Joey's mom had a hard time getting a hold of Henry because he was very scared and very wet. Finally she got him out, and all the way into the house she kept saying, "My poor, poor Henry. I am so sorry, Henry. Poor little Henry snookums."

"What is a 'Henry snookums'?" I thought to myself, but it was not a good time to ask that question.

After Joey's mom finished with Henry, she came back out to Joey and me. She told us that dropping Henry in the pool was like someone dropping us in the water when we couldn't swim. I got what she meant right away. Joey and I both felt very sad for Henry. After that we decided to just play moon games. I wasn't so crazy about pools, anyway!

Chapter Five

"JEREMY, HURRY UP, YOUR TURTLE PANCAKE IS GETTING COLD," called my mom.

I was having a lot of trouble getting my socks on and I couldn't find the shirt that was sitting on my bed just before I went to sleep. It was the morning of the first day of kindergarten. Mom came up the stairs to see why I wasn't ready and then I could hear my dad saying that he would help me. Soon, my whole family was standing in my room, including Jacob, who was supposed to be out the door going to his own school.

"Jeremy, cool pants but where's your shirt, buddy?" asked Jacob.

"Jeremy, let me help you with that other sock," said my dad as he bent over to help me.

Then Mom came rushing into my room. "Jeremy, I put all your clothes out for you last night. Where can they be? Clothes don't just walk away."

While Dad put my socks on, Mom shuffled through my bed and found my shirt rolled up under my sheets. She did not look happy when she found it.

"What's the big deal?" I thought to myself. "I can do this if everyone will just leave me alone and stop rushing me."

Before too long we were at breakfast, and Jacob, who was perfectly dressed, rushed out the door to his school. The shirt that I had on looked like one big wrinkle. Mom wanted to iron it but I said, "No. I want to wear it just the way it is." Sometimes I can be really, really stubborn. This was one of those times.

When we got to school I was the only one in the family who was not excited. Mom brought the video camera to tape my first day and my dad kept trying to get me to meet any kid he could find. The only problem was that all the other parents were doing the exact same thing. It was no fun at all.

I was assigned to the Little Hippos and for the rest of the year I would be a Little Hippo. That really bothered me because I was a little chubby and sometimes I felt like a "little hippo." Now I would be called one! Dad picked up on it right away and I could hear him in a much-too-loud voice asking Mom why a teacher would ever call a bunch of kids "Little Hippos" and Mom whispering to Dad to be quiet.

Finally, my teacher, Mrs. Moore, kicked all the big hippos out and asked all the Little Hippos to get in a circle. Out of the corner of my eye I noticed the girl who had been talking at me when I came to see kindergarten back in June.

"Hi, Jeremy," she called out really loud, which made the teacher look over at us. "Oh, Jeremy, how nice that you know someone in the class," Mrs. Moore called out, and all the other Little Hippos looked over at us as if we were buddies. So that was how kindergarten began, and for the rest of the year it was kind of just like that. Her name was Ellie and every place I went Ellie seemed to follow. Ellie was one big pain and I was *so* happy that I did not have an Ellie at home.

I liked my new class okay, I guess. There were still teacher-helpers so I was not the last one getting into my class anymore. That was good for me but not so good for the boy and girl who *were* the last.

The one thing I didn't like was when all the kids grabbed for what I had. The dinosaur table was my favorite, but the kids kept taking all the dinosaurs that *I* wanted. There were no quiet places to play and besides, we didn't get to play as much as we did in preschool. There were a lot more rules in kindergarten.

"Rules, shmules!" I didn't understand why I couldn't just make up moon games and plan my life on the moon. I might become some famous "moon" scientist someday.

We did a lot of cutting and writing in kindergarten. I still had a lot of trouble with the cutting and I was always missing part of what I was supposed to be making, just like in preschool. If it was supposed to be a square, it looked like a triangle. If it was supposed to be a ball, I saw a half moon. I just never made it right. As soon as I saw the scissors come out, I figured it was not going to be a good morning.

I already knew most of the letters in the alphabet because Mom used to play a card game called Alphabet Fish with me. But I didn't have to find the letter in kindergarten: I had to draw it. Each time I tried to make a letter, Mrs. Moore kept talking about having my letters look in a different direction. I wanted to tell her that letters were not people so they can't look! What was she talking about? Even drawing a letter was hard in school. "School is just not for me!"

One day a new lady came into our classroom to meet me. She was not a teacher but had two fancy big letters for her job. One was "O" and the other was "T." Her name was Miss Jill. I guess her other name was "O.T.," so that made her Miss Jill O.T.

At first Miss Jill just liked watching me cut and make my letters and play. Then one morning my mom said she was taking me to school so she could meet with Miss Jill. I corrected my mom and told her that her name was really Miss Jill O.T. Mom started to laugh really loud and then she told me that O.T. was the name of Miss Jill's job. Mom called her an Occupational Therapist.

"What is that?" I asked, feeling a little scared that it was something really bad.

"She works with children who have motor difficulties, Jeremy, which is a fancy way of saying that she is going to help you become a better cutter and writer," said Mom.

"I don't have a motor in me so why do *I* need her help?" I kept thinking to myself.

When Miss Jill came into the room where we would be working together, she showed me all the things that I would be doing with her. Some of them looked hard.

Miss Jill had all kinds of tricky things in her room, some that I had never seen before. Her rule was that she would pick the things I could play with. While I played, she and Mom talked, and I could see her showing my mom some special paper, which my mom had to write on.

Miss Jill asked me to come and sit with her and Mom for a few minutes, and then she told me that I was going to be able to come and play in her room two mornings a week. She sounded really excited about it but I was not as excited as she was. I was still worrying that I had a motor in my body somewhere that nobody told me about.

At dinner that night I was not happy when Mom told Dad and Jacob that I was going to get to see Miss Jill and play in her special room beginning the next week. Jacob got so excited for me that I was thinking maybe *he* should go. He might like it better than me. When Jacob started asking all kinds of questions about Miss Jill's room, I was not happy.

"Why do my parents always have to report to Jacob about my school?" I wondered. "It is so much more fun to eat at Joey's house. He gets to eat his dinner without having to talk about school and he doesn't have a big brother who keeps asking silly questions. Joey wouldn't like dinner at my house. That's for sure."

Chapter Six

FOR HALLOWEEN WE WERE ALLOWED TO DRESS UP IN OUR COSTUMES and parade around the school so that everyone could see what we looked like. At first I didn't want to do it, but then Joey said that he thought it was a fun idea and that he was going to do it at his school, too. Joey even gave me the idea of being a "moon man," so I asked Jacob if he could help me with the costume. I was afraid Jacob would think it was stupid, but he didn't. He spent one whole Saturday working on it with me. The costume was really awesome. Around my head were stars on sticks that came from my neck and stood straight up. Jacob even put glitter on them so they would sparkle. I looked just like the man in the moon or a "moon man" as Joey and I would say.

When I got to school, Mrs. Moore helped me put my costume on. It took kind of a long time. Some of the kids told me I looked weird, but Mrs. Moore said it was a very creative idea. I even told her that Joey and I were going to the moon on vacation someday. She didn't answer, but she did smile at me.

School was still really hard and everyone kept telling me to try my best. They kept asking me to say things over and over again and to say them more slowly. Yikes! If I talked any slower the words would forget to come out! I was trying my best but I guess it wasn't good enough for them. But there were five words that I could say perfectly, "School is not for me!"

We had a big vacation at holiday time and I got to play with Joey the whole week. He got this moonbeam gun for Christmas and when he pointed it at the wall, it looked like it was this wow light that had special powers. We decided it would have to go in our moon bags for when we finally went to the moon.

When I went back to school after vacation, a new lady came into the classroom and I could feel that she was watching me. After a few days she told me her name was Mrs. Zabin and that she worked with students to help them talk better. "Talk better, shmalk better!" I thought to myself. But I did like to listen to the stories she told me while I played with the dinosaurs. She told me that she had a big dog called a Great Dane and that he almost looked like a small pony. I asked her if she was allowed to ride her dog, but she said that dogs were not to ride, only ponies and horses. "Too bad," I thought.

One day, she asked me if I would like to come up and see her classroom. I really didn't want to leave my room, but I didn't want to hurt her feelings so I went. On the way up, I told her about Foolish. She asked me if I had any funny stories about him and I told her about all the things he ate that he wasn't supposed to. We both laughed really hard and she told me that I was a good dog storyteller. I thought she was a great dog story listener because she understood my whole story. That made me feel good.

We always seemed to be doing special things at my school. I didn't like the big deal they made about birthdays. When it was your birthday the teacher made you a funny hat, but first everybody got to write on it. I didn't like wearing that birthday hat and I felt that everybody was looking at me all day long and sometimes even laughing, especially the bigger kids in our school. I liked quiet birthdays.

When the snow came, we got to go outside and slide on tubes and build snowmen. That was my favorite thing all year. I loved playing in the snow. I liked to lie down in it and pretend I was a "Snow Superman" and could fly to the moon. I would close my eyes and pretend that I was right up there in space. I made a few friends in my new school but I never played with them outside of school and that was okay. Some of them went to aftercare and I got to see them all day long, so I didn't need to see them more. I would just wait until the weekend so that Joey and I could play together.

Dinner was like still being in school. We had to talk about every single little thing that happened in our day and most of the time I just pushed my peas around my plate and listened to Jacob. Every once in a while Mom would look at Jacob and touch her finger to her lips to give him the "be quiet" sign so that I would have a chance to talk. "It's okay," I would say. "I like listening to Jacob."

"Wrong!" I just wanted to eat in peace, but dinner was always like school in our house. I *really* liked going to bed because it was quiet there and nobody asked me any questions.

After the snow melted we went on a school trip to a farm. Mrs. Zabin came, too. She asked me if she could sit with me on the bus and she told me all about the farm we were going to visit. She said that she used to take her own boys there when they were little.

Ellie sat in the seat in front of me and kept listening to the things Mrs. Zabin asked me and then gave the answer. "Ellie the pain" is what I wanted to call her, but I didn't. Finally, Mrs. Zabin asked Ellie to let me answer.

The farm was so cool and we got to go inside a fence and pet all sorts of animals, including a little piglet. His skin was so soft and his tail had a funny curl in it. The goats were kind of a pain, like Ellie, so I didn't stay around them too long. After snack, it was time to get on the bus and go back to school. I was so tired that I almost fell asleep during the ride.

I remembered that when I first started kindergarten, Mrs. Moore had told us that before the school year ended we would all be able to read at least one little book. Wrong! Every time I started to read my little book, the letters looked like they were dancing on the page. I could read the first page that had only two words on it, but lots of times I made the wrong sounds for the letters and Mrs. Moore reminded me of the right sounds. Even Mrs. Zabin worked with me on this. It's like one big rap. "Sounds and letters, sounds and letters. You have to learn them so you can read better!" It was such hard work and so boring.

Jacob pumped me a lot about school at dinner but I didn't want to tell him that I could read a little. I was scared he would ask me to read one of *his* books. Mom and Dad didn't ask me much about school anymore. All they said was, "Jeremy, how was your day?" or something weird like that. They knew that even though school was okay, I never had a really good day there because it is too hard for me.

I was getting really excited about school ending. Even though Joey would be away for a lot of the summer, we would still have a little time to play. Besides, I was happy about not having to do sounds and letters, at least for a while.

Chapter Seven

WE TOOK OFF FOR THE BEACH AS SOON AS SCHOOL ENDED AND ONCE again, Jacob and Mom tried to give me swimming lessons, which were more like sinking lessons. Jacob even started the rap again, but Mom told him he had to stop right away! "Thank you, Mom!"

One day a boy came and sat down next to me while I was making sand castles. Instead of asking me a lot of questions, he just sat there working on his own sand castles. Each time the waves came and knocked them down, we would both start laughing. We stayed there until the tide came in and our mothers made us move. I found out his name was Donny. Each day we went to the beach I played with Donny, and each time we played we hardly talked. Even Jacob left us alone. When our vacation was over, I was sad to leave Donny and hoped that I would see him the next summer. I had two friends, Joey from home and Donny from the beach.

The rest of the summer was all about day camp and on the weekends trying to learn how to ride my bike. Oh how I hated those bike lessons. Every weekend the bike would come out of the garage, and Dad and Jacob would coach me. Mostly, Dad held me while Jacob did the coaching. And when summer ended, I still could not give up my training wheels. I was just as happy with a four-wheeler, but everyone else wanted me to be riding a two-wheeler. Everything was always about what everyone else wanted and never about what I wanted.

Joey was away most of the summer again, so we didn't really get together for a play date until right before school started. Joey got a really cool computer game from his aunt. It was about these aliens who found two spaceships. They were trying to break the code so they could use them to travel into outerspace. I was one spaceship and Joey was the other. It was so much fun.

When I wasn't playing with Joey, I just hung out and made up games with my moon men. One day Mom said that Joey could come over to our house and after lunch she took us to the library, where they were showing a movie called *School Buddies*. I guess my mom thought it would help me get excited about school starting because in a few days I would be a first grader. Wrong! The movie only made me want summer never to end.

Jacob made a big deal out of the start of school because he was going into fifth grade. He just thought he was so important. For me it was just another day and I hated that all my clothes had to be new. For the first time I'd have class the whole day, but then I still had to go to the aftercare room again when school was over. Mom said I only had to go to aftercare three days because she had decided not to work so much. I was really excited about that. I loved going home after school and lying on the rug with Foolish. When I told Foolish I would be home on Tuesday and Thursday afternoons, he started to wag his tail. He looked very happy.

Mom and Dad walked me to school on the first day of first grade like they had all the other first days of school. I wasn't sure why they both had to come, but they always did. I was happy that Jacob had started school the day before and was already out of the house.

My first-grade teacher was a man and his name was Mr. Tenny. He was really, really tall. Outside our room above each coat hook was a drawing of a brown bear. We would be known as Mr. Tenny's Brown Bears for the rest of the year. That was a lot better than last year when I was a Little Hippo.

Inside the classroom we each had our own desk, the first time for me. Written across the top of the desk next to my name were the alphabet and the numbers from one to ten. Mr. Tenny called in from the doorway and reminded us to be sure to bring our snacks in and put them in our desks.

The boy and girl who sat on either side of my desk were new to school. They looked very scared and Mr. Tenny said it was frightening to be in a new school and a new class. The boy, Dan, had just moved into our town. When he introduced the girl, Becca, Mr. Tenny showed us on the map a place called Iceland and said that she had come all the way from there on an airplane to go to our school. I felt bad that she had to fly so far to get home from school each day, but I guessed Becca didn't have very good schools where she lived.

Before the day was over Mrs. Zabin, my speech teacher from last year, and Miss Jill, my O.T., came to the class to say hello. I was really glad that they didn't stop at my desk and I kind of put my head down when they walked by. I heard them say "Hi Jeremy," but I didn't answer. I just smiled.

Mr. Tenny talked a lot about reading and writing to us. "Reading, shmeading!" I thought to myself. "Here we go again."

Mr. Tenny seemed all fired up about school and he said that he just loved being a teacher. "I sure don't love being a student!" I thought to myself, but I guess it was a good thing that Mr. Tenny liked what he was doing.

At dinner, I told Mom and Dad and Jacob about Becca and the airplane she had to go on each day to come to our school. Jacob started cracking up and Mom looked over and gave him a bad look.

"Come on, Mom. It's really funny. Jeremy thinks she flies in here everyday. How funny is that?" Jacob said.

Then Dad took over and explained to me that Mr. Tenny didn't mean that Becca did that everyday. Only the first time she came to our town from Iceland. Then he explained that sometimes people move here from really far-away places and they have to fly with all their stuff. Jacob was still laughing and snorting across the table, but finally he stopped those awful noises.

By the end of the first week, Mr. Tenny had all the Brown Bears under control and I liked him a lot. If someone was not being good at their seats, he would just stop talking and stare at them. Pretty soon they would stop. Dan, the new boy, who sat next to me, was a big talker so he got those looks a lot.

One day, a new teacher named Mrs. Davis came to get me and Dan. She said that she was a reading teacher and that she was going to do some reading activities with us that she thought we would enjoy. Her room was as big as our regular classroom and had these big round tables in it. There were posters all over about reading and books. Dan started touching everything in her classroom and even pulled a thumbtack out of a poster. Then, when we sat down at her table, Dan wouldn't be quiet. Finally, Mrs. Davis took out a box of little plastic bears. She gave four to me and four to Dan and she told us that each time we wanted to talk we had to give her one of our bears. Once the bears were gone, we couldn't talk anymore except to answer her questions. Poor Dan used up all his bears right away and then he had to sit and be quiet. He looked like he was going to pop, but pretty soon he started to listen more. "Maybe Mom and Dad should get some of those bears for Jacob," I thought to myself.

Mrs. Zabin kept working with me on my sounds and letters. She taught me how to say things that were hard for me to get out on my own. She always spoke perfectly, but a lot of the time she was not sure what I was saying, so we had to work on speaking slowly and carefully. She wanted my words to come from way down deep inside. Sometimes they were so deep that I couldn't find them until Mrs. Zabin helped me out.

We had to write a lot more in first grade. When I went to see Miss Jill, she asked me to copy words and letters from her special book. I had to sit up really tall and put my arm on the desk the way Miss Jill did. I had this big fat pencil that I had to hold a special way. If I did a good job, I got a sticker to add to my sticker book. The stickers were okay. The writing was hard work and it took me a long time to do it.

I was really happy when November came and we had a holiday from school. Most days I was so tired that I just wanted to take a nap when school was over. Twice I fell asleep in aftercare. The new boy, Dan, went to aftercare, too. Sometimes he asked me if I wanted to play with him and I did. But at times he wasn't very nice to me and I just said, "I don't think so. Not today, Dan."

Right before Christmas Mrs. Davis told me that she wanted me to work harder in reading. She said that I was really smart and that if I worked just a little bit harder, she was sure I would be reading on my own very soon. "Harder, shmarder!" I thought to myself. "Here we go again. I *was* trying really hard but I just couldn't remember all the things that I needed to. Everything got all mixed up in my head and the letters moved around a lot and made me lose my place."

The one thing I was good at was math. I liked using numbers. It was a lot quicker for me than reading. Mr. Tenny called on me for the answer all the time and he said that he liked the way I was a good math thinker. Becca was also a good math thinker, and sometimes he would put Becca and me at the back table and we would do extra math. I felt smart in math after that. Even though Jacob said that girls were weird, I liked working with Becca, but sometimes I couldn't understand what she said. She talked too fast. If I gave her a funny look, she would say it again, so I had to give her a lot of funny looks.

When February vacation came, it snowed almost the whole week and Jacob and I built all kinds of snow forts. Mom called to see if Joey could come over, but no one was home. Then one day she asked me if I wanted to play with Dan. I kind of didn't, but I guess Mom wanted me to because that afternoon he came over.

Jacob called him "a human bulldozer" because Dan took everything apart, including all our snow forts. Lunch was the best. Dan brought a snowball in from outside and dropped it in his hot cocoa when Mom wasn't looking. It melted and cocoa spilled everywhere. Mom did not look happy, at least not until Dan's mom came to pick him up. When he left, Mom said she needed some quiet time, and Jacob and I got to watch TV for almost two hours. Jacob said we were really lucky that day. That was the only time Dan ever came over to my house.

After February vacation, I began to see Mrs. Davis by myself, without Dan. She and I started to do some new things that she called reading exercises. I always thought exercise was something people that have a lot of energy do, but maybe there are other kinds. Anyway, each time I went up to her room she asked me to look at different things and answer questions about them. Then she wrote my answers down, but she didn't allow me to see them. A few times she didn't talk, but a mystery person from a tape recorder did. Sometimes I didn't even have time to give her my answer and she told me the time was up and I was all done. "All done?" I thought to myself. "I didn't even get started!"

Just before school ended, Mom and Dad told me they were coming to my school to have a meeting about my work. I wished they didn't tell me that because it made me really worried. Maybe I wasn't smart enough to go to second grade. Maybe I would have to move to another new school. Besides, why wasn't *I* going to the meeting? It was all about *my* work, not theirs.

After the meeting, Mom and Dad stopped in to see me in my classroom. I wanted to hide under my desk. What were they thinking? Dan wanted to know why they were there and pretty soon everybody looked as if they wanted to know, too. No other parents were in our classroom, just mine! Finally, Mr. Tenny told them that it was time for us to go to gym. As soon as he said that, Mom and Dad left. Thank you, Mr. Tenny!

A few weeks later, when Jacob was out for an overnight at a friend's house, Mom and Dad said we could get pizza. At first I was very excited to have pizza for dinner, at least until they started talking about school. They told me that on some of my work that they called "testing" I did a great job, but on other things, I might need some extra help.

"Duh!" I thought to myself. "I've been getting extra help since preschool. What's so new about that?"

Dad tried to explain to me that I was really smart and that, with help, I would do better. He used these big words, "learning problems." Mom looked really annoyed when Dad said them to me, so I think they are something really bad. I liked having pizza but I didn't like any of the dinner talk at all that night.

On the very last day of school, we had a picnic outside. We played games almost the whole day and then we got to make our own ice cream sundaes after lunch. You should have seen Dan's sundae! It was falling out of the dish and there was marshmallow topping and sprinkles falling everywhere. Then instead of using a spoon, Dan put his mouth into it and he got marshmallow topping on his eyebrows. Mr. Tenny did not look happy. He gave Dan a lot of napkins and a spoon and told Dan that ice cream sundaes had to be eaten with a spoon.

When it was time to say goodbye, we gave Mr. Tenny a T-shirt that had all our names on it. I had trouble writing on it, so I wasn't sure he'd be able to read my name. I hoped he could because I liked Mr. Tenny a lot. I even liked school a little bit better.

Chapter Eight

THAT SUMMER WE ONLY WENT TO THE CAPE FOR TWO WEEKS. FOR the first time ever, it rained almost the whole time we were there. We saw a lot of movies and went down to a place called Woods Hole and learned about the ocean. But each night when we went to bed, our sheets were really cold and damp. Mom said the bad weather was doing that.

When Dad joined us for the second week, every morning he would say, "I'm sure we're going to get a winner today," but we never did. It just rained and rained and rained. Once we even lost power, so we packed up and went home a day early. Even Jacob was glad to leave. I know I sure was, even though it meant that it was almost time for me to start camp.

I was going to the camp I had gone to last summer, which didn't excite me too much. But on the first day, this really big guy came up to me and told me his name was Mo and that I was going to be in his group. His counselor partner was Joe and they said they were the Mo and Joe team. Mo seemed so happy to have me in his group that even *I* got excited about it. Mo smiled all the time and he never asked me one question, which made me like him a lot. Sometimes, while Joe was teaching the kids in our group stuff that I didn't care about, like some big sports game, Mo would come and sit with me and tell me about himself. I think he must have been a lot like me when he was little. He told me that when he was my age school was hard for him and that he didn't have a lot of friends. It sounded like me, but I didn't want Mo to know that.

One day, when it was Mo's turn to run the game, he looked over at me and asked me to be his helper instead of Joe. At first I wanted to say, "No way," but then he told me what he needed me to do and it seemed pretty easy so I got up and helped him out. After that, the other kids thought I was this really important guy and sometimes when they asked Mo a question, he would look at me and say, "What do ya think, boss man? Should we let them have ten more minutes of free play?" "Sure, why not," I would answer, and then all the kids would yell out, "Thanks, Jeremy!"

When it was time for swimming lessons, I think Mo talked to the swimming instructor because she let Mo come in and help me. His hands were so big I think he could have held me up with one finger. For the first time ever, I held my breath under water and I wasn't scared like before. I even stayed up alone and floated. Mo told me that I was doing a great job and that I would be swimming on my own the next summer in camp.

Before too long I couldn't wait to get to camp each day and see Mo. After the first week I even started to talk to some of the kids in my group. When they spoke to me, Mo would say, "Hey there, Jeremy, you have to answer them, buddy," so I did. Before that I used to just listen and I didn't think anybody cared much about my answers.

At dinner I told Mom and Dad all about Mo and Joe. Even Jacob said that he wished that he had them for his counselors. That was a first! After that, Jacob asked me each night at dinner how the Mo and Joe show was going and we would all laugh.

At the end of camp, for the first time in my life, I got this amazing award. It was the Future Camp Counselor Award for a camper who shows he can lead a group by himself. It was a picture of our group with me in the front between Mo and Joe. All the kids had signed their names on the sides of the picture. I remembered the day the picture was taken and how Mo and Joe had asked me to move more toward the center of the picture. At first I didn't like being right up front where everybody could see me, but then Mo said he needed me there because he didn't like having his picture taken very much. I think it was a trick to get me to stand in the front.

When camp ended and Mo said goodbye to me, I was very sad. Mo told me that I always needed to remember that "doing my best" was about doing what was good enough for me and not to worry about the other kids. He made me promise that I would never forget that. He also told me that maybe I'd grow up to be a big guy like him and that he liked who he was. When he gave me five and said goodbye, he thanked me for making his summer job so special. As I walked away, I kept thinking that maybe *I* should have thanked *him!*

Chapter Nine

JOEY CAME BACK FROM HIS SUMMER VACATION JUST BEFORE SCHOOL started. Mom invited Joey and his mom to go to the beach with us, and Jacob brought his friend Anthony along. The beach was kind of far from our house, but I liked it a lot. Jacob and Anthony went out and played on the sandbars while Joey and I spent the whole day on the beach making sand castles. I was happy that he didn't ask me to go swimming. We just ran in and out of the water. A few weeks later we had another play date and this time I got to go to Joey's house. Then, before I knew it, it was almost time to start school again. I wasn't excited at all about second grade.

Jacob always said, "Bigger grade, bigger work." "School is just not for me," I would be thinking to myself.

When it was time to start second grade, my family stopped making a big deal of the start of school and it was more like any other day. I liked that a lot better and I was starting to feel okay about not doing as well as Jacob in school.

"Maybe Mom and Dad decided they had one really smart son and one that was just a little bit smart," I thought to myself.

Mom and Dad still came with me on the first day and I still had the new school bag and the new sneakers. But they finally let me wear what I wanted and not some new stuff that I didn't even pick out.

My teacher met us at the door. She was new to the school and I heard Mom tell Dad the day before that she could not figure out why they would give me a new teacher. I think what she was really saying was, "Why would they give someone with all his problems to a new teacher?"

Miss Hatsis was not young at all like I thought she would be, but she wasn't old either. She was kind of in the middle.

"Good morning, Jeremy. Welcome to second grade," she said as she put out her hand to me. "I'm very excited about being in your school and being your teacher."

I was hardly listening to her because I was trying to figure out how she knew my name. That did not give me a good feeling at all. "I must be some famous 'dumb' student that everyone knows about," I thought to myself.

"I bet you're wondering how I know who you are, Jeremy," said Miss Hatsis. "If you come inside I'll show you." Inside the door was an easel and on it were small pictures of each of the kids in the class.

"I borrowed these from the office files because I am new to the school and I wanted to be able to put a face to a name right from the start," said Miss Hatsis. "I think your desk is over there."

I liked Miss Hatsis right away and I had a better feeling about second grade than I had had about first. She didn't gush over me. She just let me do my thing the way I did it. At least she made it seem that way.

Every day Miss Hatsis read with each one of us separately. She divided us into three reading groups, but they weren't groups of all good readers and then the medium readers and finally the bad readers, like me. They were all mixed-up groups. We still had phonics books, except I didn't do the same pages as everybody else. That kind of bothered me, but their pages were much harder than mine so maybe it was okay.

One day Miss Hatsis asked me if she could tape record my reading. That was the first time that anyone thought I was good enough to tape. She told me that once a month she was going to do that if it was okay with me. She even told me that when there was time, she would play it back for me but not in the very beginning.

Then Miss Jill and Mrs. Davis stopped in to see me the second week of school. Miss Jill said that she would only be seeing me once a week and Mrs. Davis said that a new teacher named Mrs. Horton was going to be working with me instead of her. Mrs. Davis said she was still interested in what I was doing but that she didn't work with second graders.

I knew about Mrs. Horton because she had called my mom just before school started and told her that she was going to be my resource teacher and that she would be helping me just as Mrs. Davis had. Mom said she was called a "resource teacher" because she had all these things that would help me called "resources." "TMI (too much information)," I thought to myself.

Anyway, her name was Mrs. Horton. In the beginning, she just came to my classroom and read with me or helped with my phonics and my writing. Then one day she asked me to go for a walk with her up to her room.

On the way up she pointed out that there was a yellow line of tiles in the middle of the floor. It was on every floor of our school and students were asked to line up on the yellow line whenever we were going or coming from somewhere in our building. Mrs. Horton told me that whenever students went up to her room, she began by asking them to follow the yellow tile line until they got to her door. She made it seem like a real adventure.

"Jeremy, your mom tells me that you are really good at finding things. There is a game called a scavenger hunt that I think you will enjoy and it is all about finding things. Someone makes up a list of things that you need to find, and you go off and find them. From now on, when you come into my room, I want you to pretend that you are on a scavenger hunt and you are looking for the tools that will help you to become a better reader. So each time you come up to my room I want you to follow the yellow tile line and I want you to pretend that you are hunting for the tools that can make great things happen for you in reading. Do you think you can do that, Jeremy?" Mrs. Horton asked. I just smiled but I didn't answer. I wasn't sure what to think about it all, but I already knew that I really liked Mrs. Horton a lot.

As we followed the yellow tile line, we talked about lots of different things. I liked that instead of Mrs. Horton asking me a lot of questions. She told me all about her dog and all the things she liked to do in her free time. Even though I wasn't sure of what I would see in her classroom, I was okay with going there.

Her room was very different from my classroom. I could tell Mrs. Horton liked her space because she kept showing me all the things in it. Finally, it was time to sit down and work. But instead of starting to work, she said, "Jeremy, I have been listening to your reading on the tape that Miss Hatsis did. I am very impressed with how hard you are working at reading. I was wondering if I could just ask you to do something for me."

"Yikes, it was always the same," I thought to myself. "Everyone always wants me to do something for them, even though I'm not very good at anything I do in school."

"Each time you come into my room, Jeremy, you will need to say a special password. From now on, your password to get into my room each day is going to be 'I can do it.' Do you think you can remember that?"

"I think so," I kind of whispered. Nobody had ever asked me to use a password before.

"Now let's talk a little bit about your reading," Mrs. Horton said.

In the beginning she asked me a few easy questions about reading and letters and sounds and especially about remembering. Then she told me something that no one had ever told me before.

"Reading has nothing to do with how smart you are, Jeremy, so if you are having difficulty with your reading it is not because you are not smart. It is perhaps because your filing system is off and the sounds and symbols for the letters are not being filed in the correct places. If you think of your brain as a computer, when you push the wrong button on a computer things get all mixed up.

When you are reading, lots of things can happen to the information," Mrs. Horton said.

"The information may not be going into the right place and so when you go back to get the information later on, it's still there but you can't find it. I am going to teach you how to read using a program that will hopefully get all the information in the right place for you and also help you to find it when you need it."

"Boy, that was a lot for me to try to understand," I thought, and Mrs. Horton wasn't even finished yet.

"Instead of thinking that you are not a good reader, I want you to think of yourself as someone who is going to become a great reader. Can you do that for me, Jeremy?" Mrs. Horton asked.

"I can try, Mrs. Horton," I said in a very, very low voice. I always used my low voice because I was hoping people would not hear me if it was the wrong answer.

"Wonderful, Jeremy. Now, do you remember the password?" Mrs. Horton asked.

"I can do it," I whispered.

"I can't hear you, Jeremy," said Mrs. Horton.

"Say it like you believe you can do it, Jeremy."

All of a sudden I took a really deep breath and yelled out, "I can do it!" and Mrs. Horton and I began laughing really hard.

Chapter Ten

I FOLLOWED THE "YELLOW TILE LINE" BACK TO MY CLASSROOM AND from then on I traveled that road almost every day up to Mrs. Horton's room. Sometimes she came down to my classroom and helped some of us with writing and math. Each time she sat down to work with me, she would whisper to me to remember the password and each time I would say it.

The reading help that Mrs. Horton gave me was also about letters and sounds and words and even writing sentences, but it was different from anything I had done before. I can't tell you exactly why. Mrs. Horton said that it was really important for us to do each thing each time I saw her in the very same order, kind of like one, two, three. We would begin by looking at the really special letters called vowels and I would have to name the vowel, give a special word that began with it, and then give the sound it made. Sometimes I messed up, but Mrs. Horton would always smile and say, "Try again, Jeremy," and then she would give me a hint. Most of the time, I got it.

Then we would work on the letters of the alphabet that aren't vowels, the consonants, and the sound that each of those letters makes. Next Mrs. Horton would go over what we did the last time I was there and then she would teach me something new. Sometimes I wasn't ready for something new because it was hard for me to remember it all. Mrs. Horton would always smile and remind me of the password and to just keep trying. The best part was when we made up silly words with letters that had magnets on the back and we put them on a special board. Mrs. Horton called them nonsense words and she even invented some new word games to help me. It was work and fun all at the same time, and sometimes it was a little boring, but I didn't seem to mind that much.

When I had to write the words and the short sentences that Mrs. Horton called "dictation," it took me a long time to finish. I think Mrs. Horton had trouble reading what I wrote, because she would ask me to read my words and sentences back to her and then she'd write her own words above mine. She told me she had old eyes, but I think it was because of my bad handwriting and spelling. Whatever it was, I didn't feel as bad anymore and I knew that Mrs. Horton was really proud of me. Mrs. Horton's special rules helped me to remember how to put the letters together to make the words. Slowly, I was beginning to remember the things Mrs. Horton was teaching me.

In the classroom, reading was still hard and I hated it when Miss Hatsis called on me. I felt that everyone was looking at me and thinking I was not very smart. Sometimes they looked as if they were thinking, "Why'd you call on Jeremy? He can hardly read." That's when I would remember what Mrs. Horton told me. I would keep thinking about the password and sometimes I could read most of the words without any help. But then there were the times when Miss Hatsis ended up telling me what each word said. I really wanted to be able to read all the words on my own like most of the other kids in my class.

Twice a week I went to Mrs. Zabin for speech help. Her room was near Mrs. Horton's room so I would pretend I was following the "yellow tile line" up to speech, too. I worked on different things with Mrs. Zabin and when I did a really good job, she would give me a treat out of her treasure chest. It made me want to work even harder because her treasure chest was full of neat things that I never saw before, like funny little puzzles with parts attached that all fit together in a special way.

Mrs. Zabin was helping me to remember things and to find little clues that would help me to remember. Sometimes she would ask me to name as many things as I could really fast and then she would time me. Sometimes she would read to me and ask me all kinds of questions about what she read. That was really hard because it got all mixed up in my head and I had trouble remembering what happened first and then after that and after that. But she always told me that I was working hard and doing a good job.

At home, dinner was still the same. Jacob would sit there and tell story after story about his day. One night I decided to tell Jacob and Mom and Dad about what I was doing with Mrs. Horton. I think they were really surprised that I talked about it. Of course, Jacob did not hear a thing I said because he was too busy asking me where Mrs. Horton's room was. So I told him it was at the end of the "yellow tile line" and everyone at the table started to laugh, including me! It was the second time that I could remember that dinner was funny to me and I kind of liked that I was the one who made it that way.

Chapter Eleven

DAD KEPT HELPING ME TRY TO RIDE MY BIKE WITHOUT THE TRAIN-
ing wheels and Jacob continued to be the coach. I almost did it,
but then I would get nervous and put my feet down because I
was afraid I was going to lose my balance and fall over. I knew
that Jacob was just trying to help, but I kind of wanted to try
with just Dad. Finally, one day, when my dad was putting my
bike away, I told him that I didn't like Jacob helping me all the
time. Mrs. Zabin told me that it was important to speak up and
tell people how I felt. Usually I just sat there with a grouchy look
on my face and didn't say a word. This time it felt good to tell
my dad how I felt.

At first Dad didn't say a word, he just looked at me in a funny
way. Then he got a big smile and said, "Well, Jeremy, let's see
what we can do about that!"

In late spring, when Dad was out raking leaves, I asked him if
he could get my bike out. He looked really surprised but I knew
it was safe because Jacob was going over to his friend Anthony's
house. I was really worried that Dad was going to tell Jacob that
I had asked for my bike, but instead he called out to Jacob, "Have
a great time," and then he looked at me and winked.

Once Jacob was out of sight, Dad got the bike out and took
the training wheels off. He held it steady while I got on. I
thought for sure I was going to fall off like all the other times.
Then I started to think of the password for Mrs. Horton's room
and I pretended the sidewalk was the "yellow tile line." I started
to pedal and really concentrate. At first, I was sure I was going

to fall off like all the other times, but this time, just as I started to fall, I put my foot out and held the bike up. Then I got back on and tried again. I kept saying the password over and over again and suddenly I couldn't hear my dad anymore because I was all the way down the sidewalk. After years of trying, I was finally riding my two-wheeler without training wheels. I kept riding up and down the sidewalk as fast as I could. I turned around in our neighbor's driveway. Lucky for me it went around in a half circle so I could go out the other side without stopping or getting off. When I came down the sidewalk toward Dad, Mom was outside watching and got all teary and gooey about the whole thing. It was the most exciting day of my whole life!

I spent the whole weekend riding my bike, even when it was raining. At dinner on Sunday night, Jacob asked me what it was that finally made me want to do it. I looked up at him with a big grin on my face and I said, "I could do it because I said the magic password 'I can do it' and then it happened. I can finally ride my bike without training wheels." Jacob looked very confused, but Mom and Dad seemed to understand. Finally, *I* had something special to talk about at dinner and Jacob was listening to me.

On Monday, I couldn't wait for writing to start at school because I wanted to write a story about riding my bike. Writing was usually just before lunch, so I kept watching the clock to see when it would be time. Finally, we began our work. I called the story:

JEREMY RIDES

I am not good at enyting but I reali went to be good. My techr says that I just take longor to be good at tings. I am not lik my brothr Jacob. He is good at evriting and he dose it really quick lik the othr kids.

Then one day, I got a magik pasword and each time I ust it magik tings hapent. When I got on my bikel sed the pasword to myself ovr and ovr agen.

"I can do it. I can do it. I can do it." Sudenli my bike was on the yello til line and I was on my way riding as fast as I cood.

If you are bad at tings like me, you need to use the magik pasword, two. Just say, "I can do it" ovr and ovr agen and you will be abel to do hard tings, two.

Miss Hatsis liked my story so much that she asked me to read it to the whole class. She asked everyone to tell me what *they* liked about the story and then asked if anyone had any more ideas for me. One girl named Suzie said that I should draw pictures, but I was not good at drawing. Miss Hatsis told me that if I wanted to do that and if I wanted help with the drawing that Suzie could help me. Then she asked me if I wanted to go up and read the story to Mrs. Horton and Mrs. Zabin because she thought it was so wonderful.

One of the kids in my class, Jonathan, even asked if he could go with me.

"Sure," I said, kind of wondering why he was finally being so nice.

On the way upstairs, Jonathan told me how much he liked my story. I guess that was kind of him, but I just shrugged my shoulders. Then he told me that he thought I was a really good writer.

At the end of the "yellow tile line" we went into Mrs. Horton's room and I wasn't sure what I was supposed to tell her. She looked very surprised to see me. Jonathan kind of took over and told her why we were there.

"Who's your friend, Jeremy?" she asked.

Before I could answer, Jonathan yelled out, "I'm Jonathan and Jeremy wrote a good story and Miss Hatsis wants him to show it to you."

"Jeremy, how wonderful," said Mrs. Horton. "Would you like to read it to me?"

I read the whole story to Mrs. Horton and she looked very proud of me. She even asked me to read it again and I did.

Then I knocked on Mrs. Zabin's door, but this time *I* told her about my story before Jonathan got a chance. She got so excited that even *she* wanted me to read it twice. I kept thinking to myself, "Maybe I really am smart."

After that day, I liked writing more and more. My spelling was not good, but I had good ideas, and Miss Hatsis said that was

48

the most important part of writing, your ideas and how you say them. After that it was okay for Miss Hatsis to hear me read.

She didn't say "I can't hear you, Jeremy" anymore because I read louder and tried much harder to say the words I didn't know. I wasn't good at reading but I think I was getting better. I didn't worry about what the other kids were thinking so much anymore, but I still got a tight tummy when it was my turn to read and sometimes my hands would feel kind of wet.

One Saturday, Jonathan invited me for a play date to his house. I was very surprised when Mom told me about it. At first I didn't want to go because Joey was my good friend, not Jonathan, but Mom and Dad said I could have more than one good friend and so I went.

Jonathan also had a big brother just like me and he even had two bikes in the garage so we spent the whole day on the bikes. He lived on a dead-end street so we got to ride up and down with no cars around.

I liked playing with Jonathan almost as much as I liked playing with Joey. He didn't know as much about the moon as Joey, but he knew a lot about riding bikes. My dad said that it's fun to have more than one friend and to do different things with each of them. He might be right. Jonathan liked riding bikes a lot more than Joey did and Joey liked the moon a lot more than Jonathan did. That's a good thing because I don't think we can ride bikes on the moon. At least, not yet.

When I went back to school on Monday, I didn't feel alone anymore. Jonathan talked to me right away and told me he had a lot of fun on Saturday. Nobody, except Joey, had ever said that to me before. Then some of the other kids also started talking to me. None of them had ever paid much attention to me before except for those bad looks during reading.

School was beginning to be more and more okay. When it was almost time for second grade to end and for summer to begin, I was a little bit sad. I finally stopped saying "school is not for me" to myself all the time.

Chapter Twelve

ON THE VERY LAST DAY OF SCHOOL, MISS HATSIS ASKED EACH OF us to read one thing that we had written that was special to us. Mine was a list of things that I did and didn't like about school. I had made it with Mrs. Horton way back when I first started to go to her room. Just before school ended, we made a new list and I decided to read it to my class. This was the very first time I ever shared my feelings out loud except for my bike story.

THINGS I LIKE

Walking on the yellow tile line
Not being the last one in anymore
Having a desk and not a cubby

Jonathan, my new friend
My special password that helps me do everything
My big brother, Jacob (most of the time)
Math
My dog, Foolish
Feeling smart
Joey, my outside-of-school friend
BEING ME!

THINGS I DON'T LIKE

Kids talking at me a lot
Swimming lessons
Too many teachers
Jumping words and sentences
Spelling, because it is too hard
People talking too fast
Cutting things out and missing parts
Drawing
Remembering too many things
Sounds and letters, letters and sounds

I asked Miss Hatsis if I could go last because I was scared. Most of the kids read stories they wrote. I was getting nervous that everyone was going to laugh at my list, but I kept thinking of my password and I kept saying it really quietly to myself over and over again. "I can do it, I can do it, I can do it."

I could feel the words getting all mixed up and I wanted to stop right after I began. My face was getting really hot. Then Miss Hatsis said that I could start again, but first she told the class that I had made a list of all the things that I liked about school this year and what I didn't like about school, and she told them it was okay for me to say what I didn't like.

Mrs. Horton said that we always should read the good stuff first so people will feel happy and then we can share the rest.

I took a really deep breath and then I started again and the words came out much better this time. I looked over my paper and I could see Jonathan smiling at me. I even heard some of the kids laugh when I said I liked my brother *most* of the time.

When I got to "Things I Don't Like," the room got really quiet until I started out with "people talking at me." Then I said "swimming lessons" and everybody started to laugh again because there aren't any swimming lessons in our school. I laughed, too. As I went down the list and read the other things, I could hear some of the kids say, "Same for me." And when I said "cutting things out and missing parts," they laughed again. When I was all done they clapped and Suzie even whistled with two fingers in her mouth. I never saw a girl do that before.

Miss Hatsis told the class that lots of students feel the same way as me and then she read through my lists one more time, asking everyone in my class to raise their hand if they agreed. Each time she read something, lots of hands went up in the air. I guess I wasn't the only one. I always thought it was just me that didn't like school, but it really wasn't just me. School is hard for other kids, too. Mrs. Hatsis said that smart people ask questions and that if we knew everything already she wouldn't be our teacher. She'd be out of a job! So I guess it really was a good thing that I didn't know everything about everything.

Chapter Thirteen

So that is how second grade ended for me. It was my best year ever. I played with Jonathan in school and sometimes out of school, and Joey out of school when I wasn't playing with Jonathan. I started to talk to the other kids in my class a little bit more, but sometimes I didn't know what to say to them so I just smiled and they smiled back.

Next year I will be a third grader. So now you know that I have been getting help in school for a long, long time. I think I am going to need it in third grade, too, but I am hoping I won't need as much. Mom and Dad say that help is a good thing because now I can do things in school that I couldn't do before.

I think they are right and I even like the teachers who help me. And guess what? I think they like me, too. I have learned that I can have friends in school and friends out of school. The best thing of all that I learned is that I am not only good at finding things for my mom, I am also good at finding things for myself, like what my teachers call "the tools" that help me learn better in school.

Maybe you have to get help in school, too, and maybe you are also looking for "the tools" that will help *you* learn better in school. Some of the things in my story may remind you of yourself. For a long time I didn't feel very smart and I didn't have a lot of friends. It is really hard having a big brother who does everything perfectly. But ever since the summer that Mo told me that I just need to think about what is best for me and not for other people, I don't mind Jacob anymore. "He's just looking out for himself," Mo would say.

I'm not sure why I have learning problems and my brother, Jacob, doesn't, but Mrs. Horton says that no one knows the answer to that. She told me to just think about myself and what I need, and that is just what I am trying to do. And you know what? It's working!

If you have learning problems and you have to go for help the way I do, pretend that you are on a "yellow tile line" and pretend that you are looking for the tools to help you do better. Keep telling yourself "I can do it, I can do it, I can do it," as many times as you need to until you believe that you really *can* do it. I know that it is really, really hard work and sometimes it is not as easy as just saying "I can do it." The most important thing of all is to remember that, just like me, with hard work, you *can* find the tools and you *can* learn how to do it. I never thought I would say this but now "school *is* for me," and I hope it will soon be for you, too.

Your new friend,

Jeremy James Conor McGee

About the Author

MARY MAHONY IS A RETIRED ELEMENTARY-SCHOOL RESOURCE teacher who divides her time between a suburb of Boston, Massachusetts and Woodstock, Vermont. Mary is the mother of three grown children: Breen, an architect who lives and works in New York City; Colin, Senior Director of Business Development for a Massachusetts company, who lives with his wife, Katherine, and daughter, Ella, in a suburb of Boston; and Erin, who is a pediatrician in Cambridge, Massachusetts. Mary has many interests but she especially enjoys spending time with her family and her granddaughter, Ella.

Mary spent many years working with families whose children were experiencing a variety of journeys both inside and outside the classroom. In *School Is Not For Me, Jeremy James Conor McGee,* Mary gives all of us an opportunity to view the challenges of learning through the eyes of a child.

Be sure to read
Mary's other children's books

There's An "S" On My Back,
"S" Is For Scoliosis
ISBN: 0-9658879-1-X
$14.95

Stand Tall, Harry
ISBN: 0-9658879-2-8
$14.95

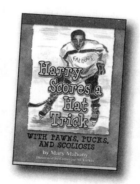

Harry Scores A Hat Trick
With Pawns, Pucks, and Scoliosis
ISBN: 0-9658879-3-6
$14.95

Mary's books can be ordered directly from her website:
www.reddingpress.com, online at amazon.com,
or at your local bookstore through Baker & Taylor.

REDDING PRESS
www.reddingpress.com